Keep Reading!!

Compliments of:

Scholastic Inc.

&

Wyoming First Lady Carol Mead

Princess Pigtoria and the Pea

by **PAMELA DUNCAN EDWARDS** ◎ illustrated by **HENRY COLE**

Orchard Books ● New York
An Imprint of Scholastic Inc.

Edwards, Pamela Duncan.
Princess Pigtoria and the pea / by Pamela Duncan Edwards: illustrated by Henry Cole. — 1st ed.
p. cm.
Summary: To make her pigsty of a palace picturesque again, penniless Princess Pigtoria
tries to get the pompous porker Prince Proudfoot to propose marriage.
ISBN: 978-0-545-15625-7
[1. Fairy tales. 2. Pigs — Fiction. 3. Princesses — Fiction.] I. Cole, Henry, 1955– ill. II. Title.
PZ8.E265Pr 2010 [E] — dc22
2008052693

10 9 8 7 6 5 4 3 2 1   10 11 12 13 14

Reinforced Binding for Library Use

First edition, February 2010

Printed in China

The artwork was created using watercolor.
The book was set in Eatwell Chubby and Eatwell Tall.
Book design by Kevin Callahan

For Margaret's princesses,
Emma and Katie Rooney, and Alex Lane.
And not forgetting the little prince, Myles.
—P.D.E.

For Princess Penni,
possibly my most preferred person.
—H.C.

rincess Pigtoria was very poor.

Her palace had peeling paint and collapsing plaster.
She planted pansies and petunias. She swept
and she polished.

"It's hopeless," she protested. "My palace
looks like a pigsty. If only I had enough pennies
to have it painted."

One day Princess Pigtoria read a personal ad in the paper.

Wanted:
A Proper Princess to become the bride of Prince Proudfoot of Porksville. Princesses must apply in person.

If I married the prince, pondered Pigtoria, perhaps
he would help me make my palace pretty again.
So, Pigtoria departed for Porksville.

Presently, Pigtoria stood in the portal of Prince Proudfoot's palace. She pounded on the door. A page led her into the presence of the prince.

PALACE
PROGRAM
Princess
Pigtoria
to arrive
precisely
at 5:00.

"So you are applying to be my bride," said Prince Proudfoot. "I am very particular. Only a perfect princess will do for someone as important as me. And you're not at all punctual. It's past supper time."

That wasn't very polite, thought Pigtoria, padding after the parlor maid toward the guest apartment.

But Pigtoria didn't know that the prince had a plan. He had placed a pea under her pillows. Only a proper princess would be prickled by a pea beneath such a pile.

"What a pity I didn't pack a picnic," sighed Pigtoria.

"We could purchase a pizza," suggested the parlor maid.

So Pigtoria picked up the palace phone.

"I'd like plenty of pizzas," she ordered, "with toppings like . . .

peppers,

Percy-the-Pizza-Pig soon appeared at Pigtoria's door.
"You're very prompt," said Pigtoria, "but, oops,
how pesky! I don't have any plates."

"No problem," replied Percy, popping off to the pantry.

Soon, in paraded the keeper of the pantry keys with paper plates and plastic cups,

the palace porter with a pitcher of pineapple punch,

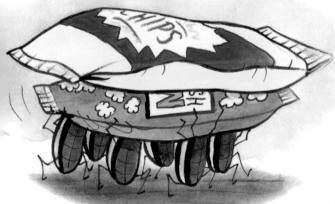

the chief potato peelers with potato chips and popcorn,

and the pastry cook with a pumpkin pie.

"Won't *you* all have a piece of pizza?" asked Pigtoria.

So Pigtoria, Percy, the parlor maid, the keeper of the pantry keys, the palace porter, the chief potato peelers, and the pastry cook ate until everything had disappeared.

Then the parlor maid played the piano and everyone performed the polka until they were pooped.

Finally, Pigtoria said,
"It's past my bedtime. We must part."

Panting, Pigtoria plunked onto her pillows. She didn't spy the pea popping out and plopping through a hole in the planks.

But Pigtoria couldn't sleep. The pizza, popcorn, and pie crumbs on her pillows

pressed through her pajamas painfully

and gave her pins and needles.

In the morning, Pigtoria went to join
Prince Proudfoot for a plate of porridge.
"I slept pitifully," complained Pigtoria.
"I have purple patches everywhere."

"Splendid!" cried the prince. "Then you were prickled by the pea I placed under your pillows. This proves you are a proper princess. You have permission to be my bride."

"YOU PUT A PEA UNDER MY PILLOWS?" exploded Pigtoria.

"I am not impressed. I could never be the partner of such a pompous prince. I much prefer Percy-the-Pizza-Pig."

"Oh, Pigtoria," cried Percy-the-Pizza-Pig, who had spent the night in the pantry pining for the princess. "Let us become a pair."

"Peachy!" cried Pigtoria.

The keeper of the pantry keys, the palace porter, the chief potato peelers, and the pastry cook clapped.

So, in April, Pigtoria put petals into her pigtail.
Percy put on his pin-striped suit and porkpie hat.

"You look like a proper prince," whispered
Pigtoria as the preacher pronounced
them pig and sow.

Pigtoria and Percy opened a chain of pizza parlors, which proved to be very profitable.

They painted Pigtoria's palace . . .

. . . and they purchased a purple pickup.

Prince Proudfoot received no other applications from princesses, proper or not. He was so depressed that the parlor maid took pity and proposed to him.

He presently became a much more pleasant pig.

Everyone was as perfectly happy . . .

. . . as it's possible to be.

As for the pea, the pocket mouse made it into a big pot of pea soup, and she held a party for all her pals.